For Seymour Surnow

With special thanks to
Kate Klimo

Library of Congress Publication data

Kyte, Dennis
    The last elegant bear.

    Summary: Abiner Smoothie, heir to four generations
of aristocratic beardom, more than justifies the fond
hopes of his papa, Baron Beauchamp "Bobo" Smoothie, and
his mama, Penny Armstrong, American copper
heiress and actress.
    [1. Bears—Fiction. 2. Teddy bears—Fiction.
3. Aristocracy—Fiction] I. Title.
PS3561.Y75L3   1983   813'.54   [Fic]   83-9396
ISBN 0-671-47442-1

Color separations by Foss and Evers.

Printed in U.S.A.

The Last Elegant Bear

The Life and Times of Abiner Smoothie

A Last Elegant Bear Book™

Dennis Kyte

Little Simon
Published by Simon & Schuster, Inc., New York

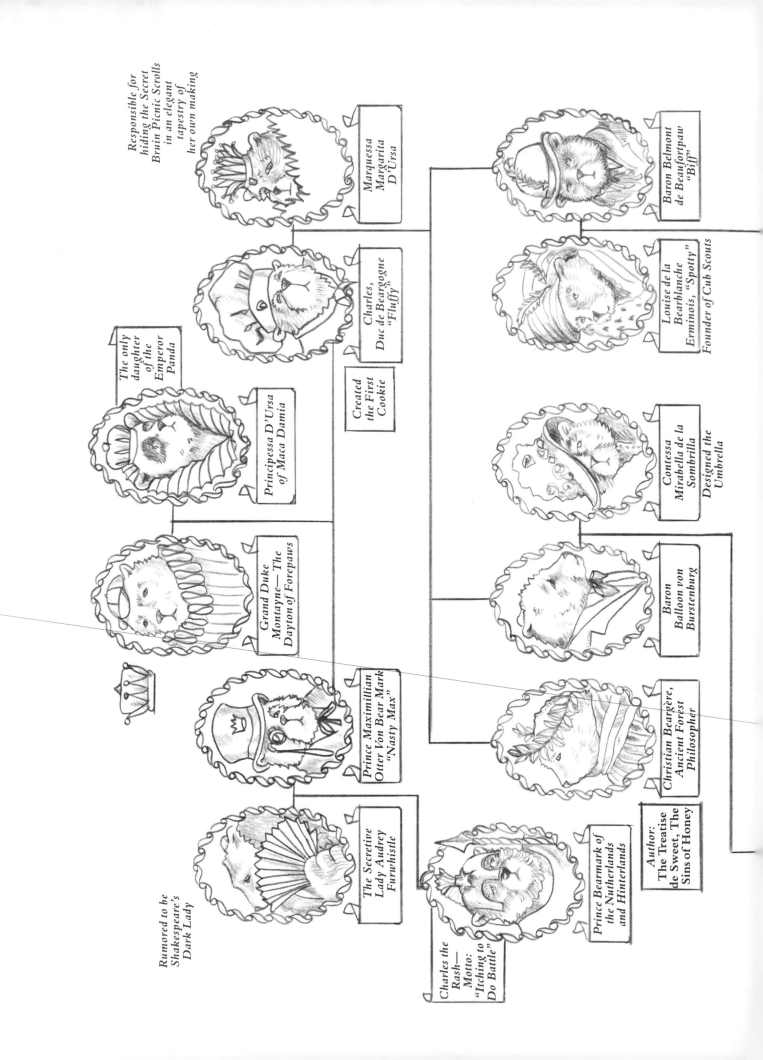

Responsible for hiding the Secret Bruin Picnic Scrolls in an elegant tapestry of her own making

Marquessa Margarita D'Ursa

Baron Belmont de Beauforpaw "Biff"

Charles, Duc de Beargogne "Fluffy"

Louise de la Bearblanche Erminois, "Spotty" *Founder of Cub Scouts*

The only daughter of the Emperor Panda

Created the First Cookie

Principessa D'Ursa of Maca Damia

Contessa Mirabella de la Sombrilla *Designed the Umbrella*

Grand Duke Montayne—The Dayton of Forepaws

Baron Balloon von Burstenburg

Prince Maximillian Otter Von Bear Mark "Nasty Max"

Christian Beargère, Ancient Forest Philosopher

Rumored to be Shakespeare's Dark Lady

The Secretive Lady Audrey Furwhistle

Author: The Treatise de Sweet, The Sins of Honey

Charles the Rash— Motto: "Itching to Do Battle"

Prince Bearmark of the Nutherlands and Hinterlands

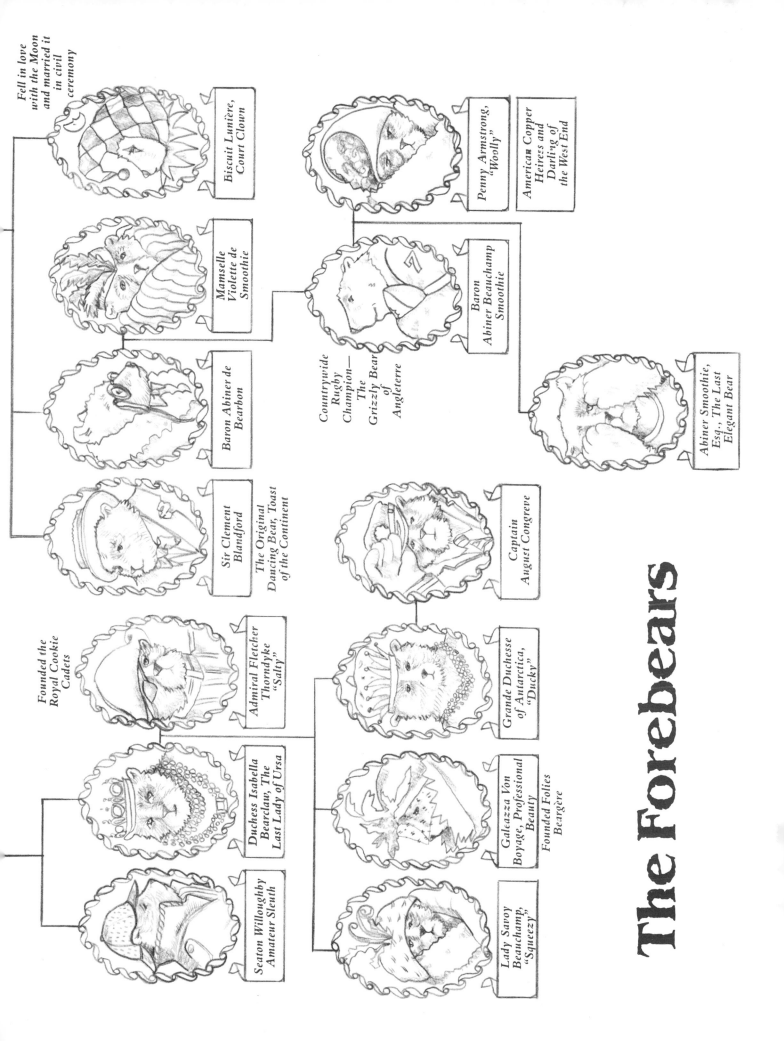

The Forebears

Fell in love with the Moon and married it in civil ceremony

Biscuit Lunière, Court Clown

Penny Armstrong, "Woolly"

American Copper Heiress and Darling of the West End

Mamselle Violette de Smoothie

Baron Abiner Beauchamp Smoothie

Countrywide Rugby Champion— The Grizzly Bear of Angleterre

Baron Abiner de Bearbon

Abiner Smoothie, Esq., The Last Elegant Bear

Sir Clement Blandford

The Original Dancing Bear, Toast of the Continent

Founded the Royal Cookie Cadets

Captain August Congreve

Admiral Fletcher Thorndyke "Salty"

Grande Duchesse of Antarctica, "Ducky"

Duchess Isabella Bearclaw, The Last Lady of Ursa

Galeazza Von Boyage, Professional Beauty

Founded Folies Beargère

Seaton Willoughby Amateur Sleuth

Lady Savoy Beauchamp, "Squeezy"

HE WAS BORN, THEY SAY, SOUND ASLEEP. SOMERSAULTING ACROSS the den rug and opening his eyes, he yawned hugely. Lively or not, everyone agreed that he was the sweetest little bundle of fur to come along in generations. What was more, the North Star was directly overhead, the moss was thick and furry, and the weather was delightfully balmy for that time of year. All in all, they told one another, it was a splendid time to come into the world.

His mama, American Copper Heiress and stage-stricken Darling of London's West End, detested long names. And so she named him shortly and sweetly—"Abiner, what else?"—and promptly went back to studying her lines for her next big part.

Abiner Smoothie he was: named for his father, Baron Smoothie, Countrywide Rugby Champion—Bobo to his teammates—the Grizzly Bear of Angleterre, and, assuredly, a gentle bear of the old school.

His paternal grandmama, Violette de Smoothie, present that day at the Smoothie country estate, Pipchippin-on-the-Harley, exclaimed upon first seeing the fluffy bundle, "But his eyes are too small!" Whereupon his American grandmother, Louelle "Bootsie" Armstrong, snatched him from her chubby clutches and examined him herself.

"Don't you people know elegance when you see it? You'd better appreciate it while you've got it; I guess this here's the last of the line," she said, kissing Abiner on his ear.

And so it was from then on, everyone would think of him as the Last Elegant Bear.

Right: Clockwise from left: Squeezy Beauchamp, his cousin; Violette de Smoothie, his paternal grandmother; Louelle "Bootsie" Armstrong, his maternal grandmother; Penny Armstrong Smoothie, his mother; Abiner Smoothie, The Last Elegant Bear, center.

Overleaf: Generations of Elegance, from left to right: Baron Beauchamp Smoothie (resplendent in a rough and tumble sort of way), Baron Belmont "Biff" de Beaufortpaw, and Baron Abiner de Bearbon, Abiner's father, great grandfather, and grandfather (respectively), pose for the renowned Master Sepia. Although he worked with a full palette, the Master's works always came out in a single color: sepia. Hence the name. Notice Abiner in the foreground. Ever the frolicsome cub, he has yet to sit still long enough for the Great Sepia to capture him on canvas. Patience, Posterity!

Clockwise from upper left, Birthdays Over the Years: Abiner on his birthday swan chair; Abiner's first mount, Chowder, with Leggins, the footman in attendance; the famous painting, "Bluebear," for which he posed with his dog, Muzzle—in his eighth year; Abiner with Great Uncle Biscuit, enjoying his annual birthday "star"; a seven-year-old Alligator and a Venetian courtier (Guess who?) share a birthday tea; Abiner and Puppy insist on blowing out the candles from the saddle.

Previous page: The Smoothie Nursery, or "Bedtime was Always a Production," starring Puppy, aloft; Mrs. Grosgrain on drums; and Abiner preparing to make the daredevil cross over to his bed. Among the playthings of this favored cub are a Noah's Ark (with animals so lifelike you'd swear they walked two by two); two indisputably real geese and a midget dromedary; and a Perpetual Christmas tree, the gift of the distinguished Master of Topiary, Douglas Fur, with the instruction that Abiner was to gaze upon it whenever he felt melancholy. The room boasted Seven Secret Hiding Places that not even Mrs. Grosgrain knew about. Notice the presence of the cookie jar, even then.

With his father off in Glass Cow at a match and his mother touring the provinces, the Smoothie household staff bids the young Master farewell as he embarks upon what many will later call some of "the Happiest Times of His Life." Abiner is thrilled about the journey that lies ahead. And what more stimulating destination than the hallowed halls of the great Paws Preparatory Academy!

As he stands before the waiting coach and five, his well-meaning but

stuffy tutor suggests that he leave Puppy in the care of Mrs. Grosgrain, whereupon Abiner narrows his already extremely small eyes and quietly growls.

From the back window of the carriage, Abiner watches as the beloved turrets of Pipchippin grow smaller and smaller. Upon his arrival at the ivy-covered walls of Paws, Abiner discovers that Mrs. Grosgrain was right when she said, in her charming Australian twang, "It won't be no bed of roses, Dearie." But it isn't bad, either.

Bidding a fond farewell, from left to right: Douglas Fur, Master of the Topiary and Fontaine, his Pachyderm Friend; old man WhiteHall, the Stuffy Tutor; Mavis, Davis, and Beatrice, the downstairs maids on stairs; Beebee, the Scullery Maid (in doorway), and in upstairs windows, upstairs maids: Sis and Miss Cranston. Leggins handles the coach and five.

IF ABINER DOES NOT DISTINGUISH HIMSELF AT PAWS PREP, NEITHER does he bring shame upon the Smoothies by being too excellent a student. Although it may not have been the intention of the Paws Prep founding fathers, Abiner finds contentment at Paws.

And why should he not? There is the monthly treat to sustain him: the unassuming little parcel that arrives on the first day of every month, covered with brown paper, tied with kite string, and filled with three dozen freshly baked cookies, each wrapped in cheerful foil by the adoring Mrs. Grosgrain, who knows just which kinds he likes. And when the cookies are all gone, there is the familiar old bathrobe, the comfortable old slippers and the sound of two plump marshmallows falling into hot cocoa at the end of each long day.

At first, the other boys are a bit standoffish. But many come to accept Abiner, particularly after he shows the pluck to sponsor his rabbit, Puppy, for membership in the Jar and Jam Club. The tougher boys are the next to come around, letting him snooze in the rugby pit afternoons when they aren't playing, and the smarter boys soon follow, letting him browse through their notes over breakfast.

But it is after school that Abiner truly blooms, rivaling his own father, the Grizzly Bear of Angleterre, himself a Paws Prep Distinguished Alum and founder of the Bruin Broozers. But no matter how many trophies crowd his bureau, Abiner is never boastful. Granted, this may be the result of generations of tasteful inbreeding. On the other hand, the Rather Slow are rarely boastful.

Right: Abiner stands on the lawn at Paws with the original Sticky Wicket. While the headmaster has specifically requested that Abiner leave Puppy in his room, Abiner carries on in his own inimitable way. Notice the Paws Prep cap lying on the grass. Abiner never did like hats.

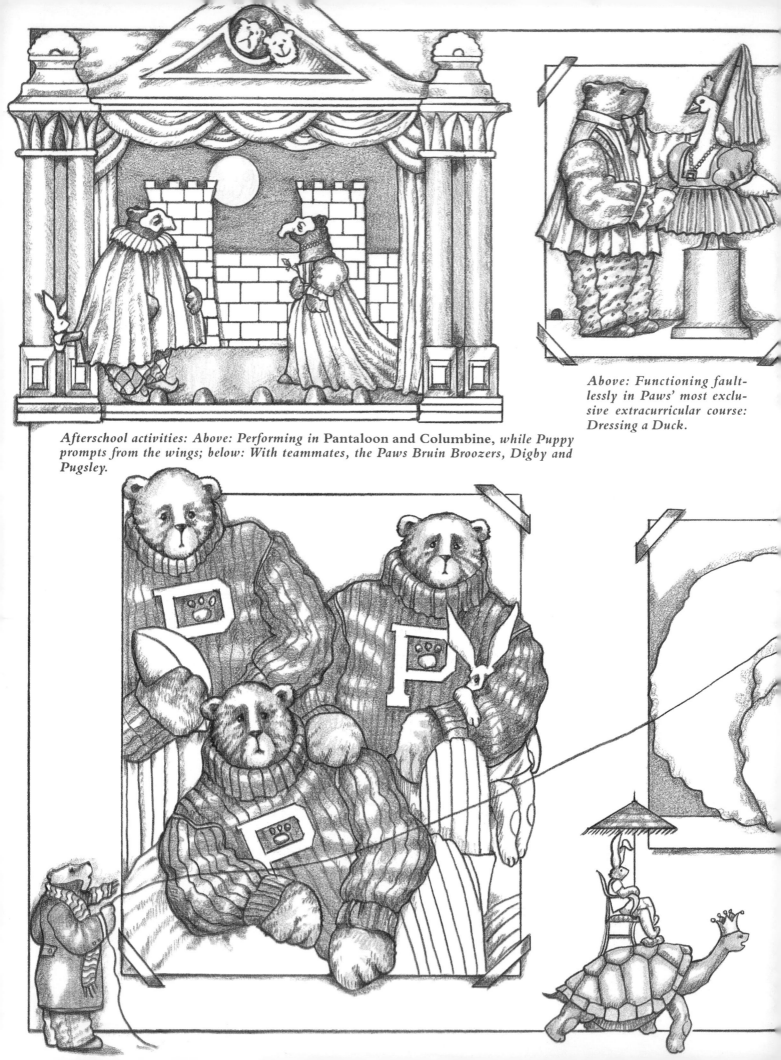

Afterschool activities: Above: Performing in **Pantaloon and Columbine**, *while Puppy prompts from the wings; below: With teammates, the Paws Bruin Broozers, Digby and Pugsley.*

Above: Functioning fault-lessly in Paws' most exclu-sive extracurricular course: Dressing a Duck.

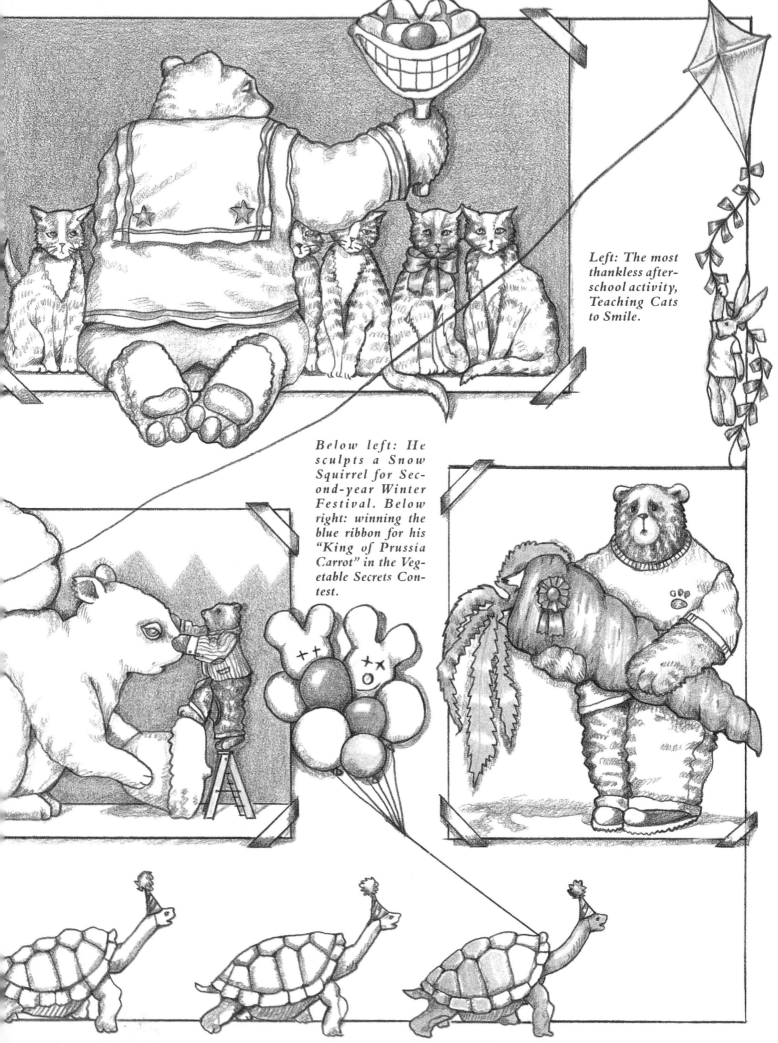

Left: The most thankless after-school activity, Teaching Cats to Smile.

Below left: He sculpts a Snow Squirrel for Second-year Winter Festival. Below right: winning the blue ribbon for his "King of Prussia Carrot" in the Vegetable Secrets Contest.

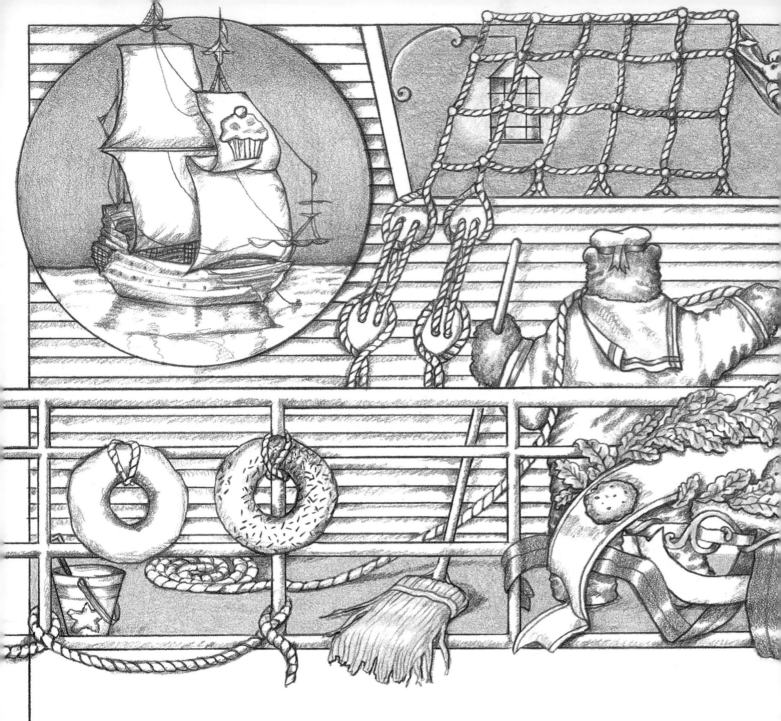

If Paws is no bed of roses, the Imperial Cookie College is even thornier. Here, an average day in the life of a cadet consists of Knot Tying (or, in Abiner's case, Not Tying); a Lecture in the History of Snacks at Sea; a course in Starboard Baking; and Rigorous Drilling in the Development of Sea Paws.

His most excellent friend while here is none other than Furbank "Teddy" Bear, a most Edwardian bear, who has been sent here by his father, the King, to learn, as his father puts it, "everything he needs to know."

Having finished learning all *he* needs to know, Abiner is sent to sea on

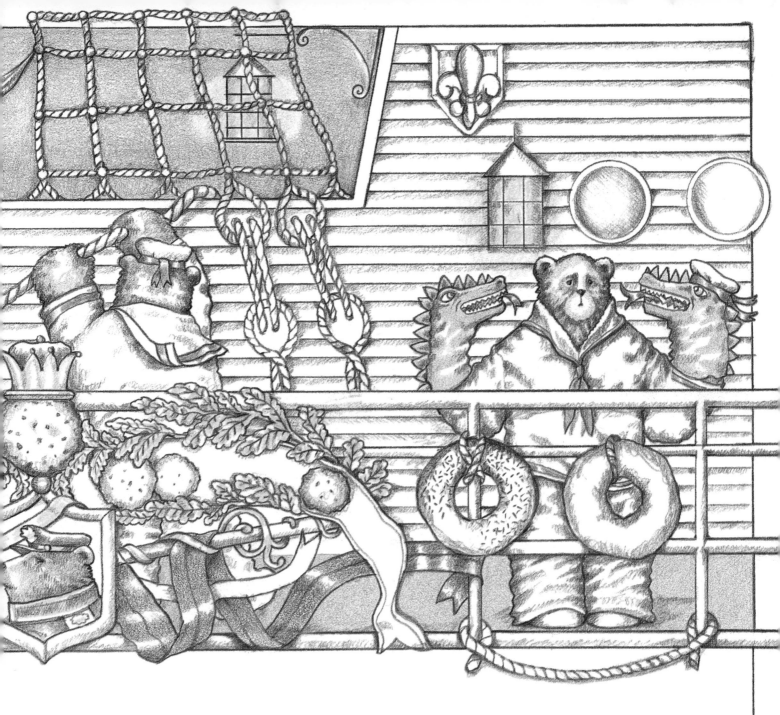

the H.M.S. *Cupcake* to put his learning to the ultimate test. His fellow officers find him to be "a little slow," and hard on the supplies, but, all in all, a worthy bear, and a gentleman. He endears himself to the mates on duty by performing puppet shows during their watch, featuring the sea serpents Minerva and Constantine. When his mates point out that there are no such things as *real* sea serpents, Abiner just growls under his breath and continues the second act.

Ensign Smoothie, as a junior officer aboard the Cupcake. *By special dispensation of His Majesty, Puppy sails as Third Mate. But poor Puppy has to be kept above deck at all times in order to avoid* mal de mer. *As hare of the dog, carrot juice and broccoli flowerets are a help, but* terra firma *is the ultimate cure.*

THE SEA RUNS, HOWEVER SLUG-GISHLY, THROUGH HIS VEINS, thanks, no doubt, to his self-appointed Aunt Ducky, the Grande Duchesse of Antarctica. And so it is that Abiner performs admirably during his tour of duty. The log testifies that he discovers for the Bruin Empire, the Lost Sea of Sagifrage. While crossing the Indian Ocean, he rescues the Seven Pink Pawed Princesses from peril at the hands of pirates. Since they turn out to be the daughters of the Wizard of The Shadow King of the Cucumber Islands, Abiner's valor is not to go unrewarded.

He returns to Port Bearsmouth and the Castle Malomar to great Pomp & Circumstance, there to be invested with the Order of the Cookie Garter. Just as he steps forward to accept this highest of honors from none other than the distinguished Admiral Fletcher Thorndyke ("Salty"), a messenger rushes in from the docks with word that a ship flying under most peculiar colors has put into port. Its captain is claiming that his holds contain gifts addressed to the "Sailor With the Small Eyes from a Grateful Wizard." Abiner signs for them, and there is no end to the bounty that is unloaded this day.

Posing for the official portrait will be the last occasion on which he will wear the actual Cookie Garter. He is soon to retire it to the Hall of Mementoes, when he himself returns to his beloved Pipchippin.

One fine spring morning of the following year, however, wanderlust strikes, as it strikes all bears in the spring, and he is off to see the world. (Or, rather, that part of the world he hadn't been able to view from the deck of the *Cupcake*.) And so, for the next year, he travels, as only can be expected, at the very height of elegance.

Right: Abiner on graduation day with gifts from the Generous Wizard: An elaborate portable lighthouse, striped, encrusted with gems, and equipped with a powerful beacon that will light the way for Lost Bears. Also pictured here is a golden casket containing seven perfect pigeon-blood ruby eggs, one from each of the grateful Princesses. At the end of graduation day, Abiner is heard to whisper to Puppy, "Before we go to bed and eat cookies let's find some peanuts for the lighthouse."

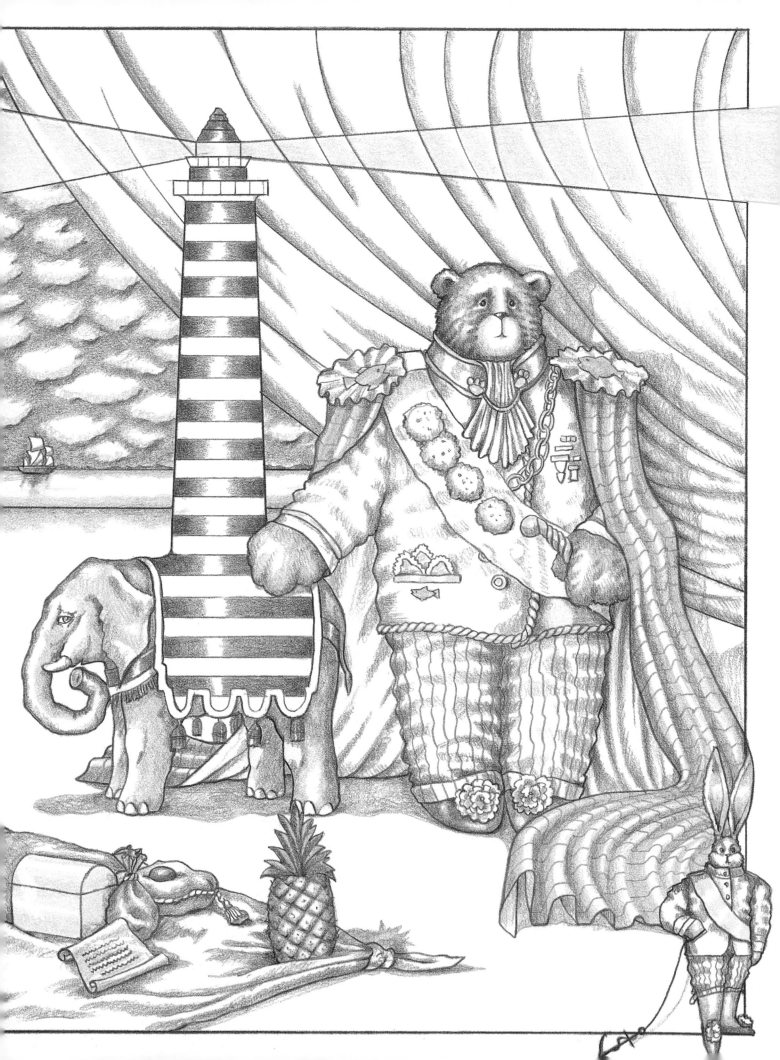

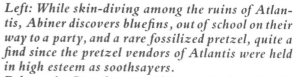

Left: While skin-diving among the ruins of Atlantis, Abiner discovers bluefins, out of school on their way to a party, and a rare fossilized pretzel, quite a find since the pretzel vendors of Atlantis were held in high esteem as soothsayers.
Below: At Stonehenge, Abiner mistakes the old ruins for a bakery and asks another tourist where they sell the eclairs.

Below: The Smoothie entourage travels the length of the Great Wall by Japanese rickshaw.

Above: A Bearble, the rare coin found in the pocket of Alexander the Great, bears the profile of Tibearius II.
Right: When in Rome....

Above: The Colussus of Quackers at sunset.
Right: Abiner and Puppy at the site where the Raven-Winged Tulip of Smoothie Crest fame was first discovered.

Below: The Tomb of the Empress Bearfurtupti, whom legend has it had a honey-coated heart.

NO SOONER HAS HE REËSTAB-LISHED HIMSELF BACK AT Pipchippin than Abiner's dear cousins Squeezy and the Glamorous Galleazza come to stay and devote the rest of their lives to his care. They know, as everyone in the family knows, that Abiner is a Bear in Need of Care. Mrs. Grosgrain, having promoted herself in Abiner's absence to Housekeeper and All-Around Major Domo, gives the Cousins the entire West Wing. Together, they come to be known as the most charming ladies in the neighboring environs. Garden Parties, Pajama Parties, Festivals, Fêtes, Balls and Gala Get-Togethers for all occasions are their specialty. Under their gracious paws, Pipchippin comes to be known as the social hub of the county. This is a good thing, too, for Abiner, ever the agreeable host, and most generous with a cookie, was never very good at organizing things.

Off-season at Pipchippin, the days are long and the shadows friendly. Mornings, Abiner takes long strolls through the gardens to talk to the topiaries, visits the Follies, and generally confuses the gardeners. After-noons are private, and for reflection and reading—everything from the writings of ancient forest philosophers to picturebooks by famous bruin artists. At twilight, he sits and sighs, waiting for the evening snack as he listens to the whisper of taffeta and secrets of the ladies in the adjoining room planning the next Pipchippin gala.

Right: Abiner reclining, contemplating the bust of a forebear in disgrace. He has never brought himself to peek underneath for fear he'll discover which branch of the tree misbehaved. The cats are none other than the Pendelton Brothers, who share everything. The mouseguest is Sasha, noted scholar of Middle-European History. The moon in the water glass is a sight too sad to be explained here. The owl is actually an ornamental Chinese Cookie Receptacle from the Ming Dynasty and a fond remnant of nursery days. The illumination at the top of this page depicts Missus Sycamore, who arrives every afternoon with her groceries to inspect the floral displays and tributes, and departs at dusk, always politely refusing tea.

Overleaf: Abiner's bedchamber, or "Bedtime is Still a Production." Abiner pauses before retiring, enjoying a little light entertainment. The Venetian Juggling Dog Circus is on first. The Dazzling Penguin String Musicians wait in the wings.

THE ELEGANT END TO EACH DAY IS THE CANDLELIT EVENING snack. The attention to detail, supervised by Mrs. Grosgrain, is scrupulous. The cookies are freshly baked and arranged on the plate, just so. The milk in a chilled goblet is placed within perfect dipping distance of the mouth. Abiner and Puppy munch, and the candle flames dance. Suddenly, they hear a whizzing overhead. They drop their cookies and look up.

It's the Chair, of course.

The chair? one might ask. There won't be a better time to bring up the Chair. The Chair is a perfectly good and comfortable chair, but at night, with dreams of being a Wingback, it has a habit of flying through the halls of Pipchippin in search of the Perfect Mirror. It is known to pose before a mirror for hours, primping and plumping its pillows, turning this way and that, and patting its skirts. It is the very essence of Vanity, this Chair.

Abiner doesn't mind, except on those evenings when he wants to sit down for a bit. When he sits where the chair *ought* to be, but isn't, he lands on the floor with a furry "plop," and sometimes growls softly.

On this particular evening, Puppy is luckily in carrot-trimmed harness when the Chair takes off in search of Itself. Always happy to indulge in a little parachute practice, Puppy makes a happy landing just as snacks are being served by the clever amphibious Monsieur Green-Oui. What gallic goodies are in store for our heroes tonight?

At right: A typical evening at home.

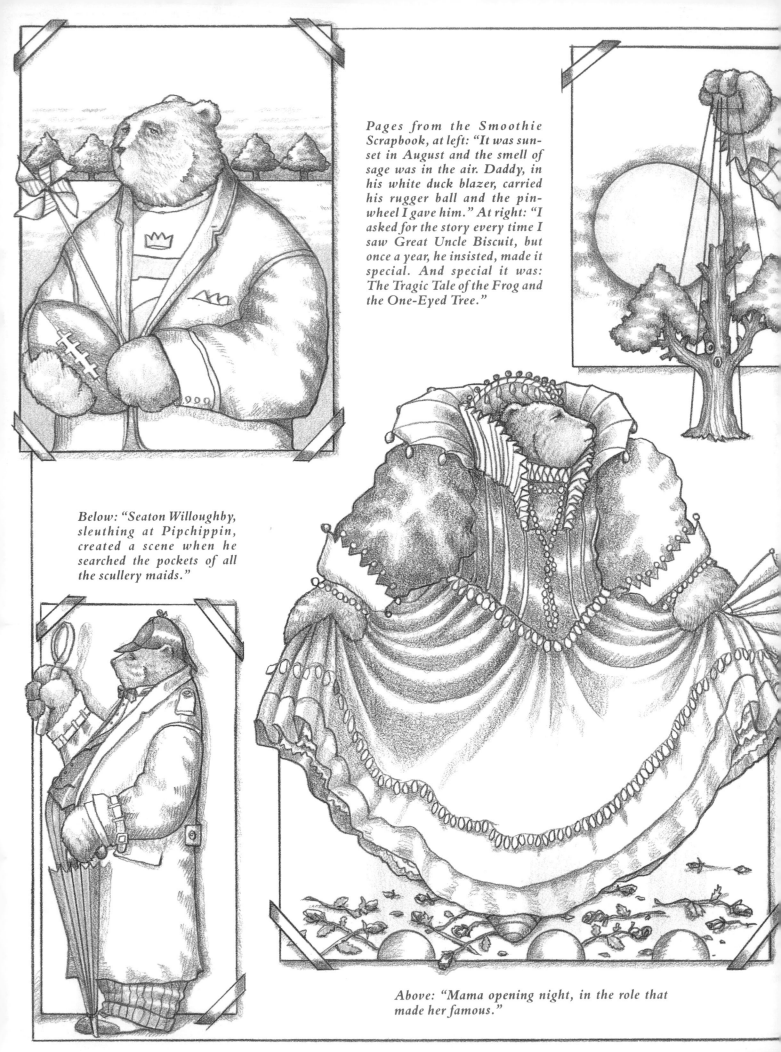

Pages from the Smoothie Scrapbook, at left: "It was sunset in August and the smell of sage was in the air. Daddy, in his white duck blazer, carried his rugger ball and the pinwheel I gave him." At right: "I asked for the story every time I saw Great Uncle Biscuit, but once a year, he insisted, made it special. And special it was: The Tragic Tale of the Frog and the One-Eyed Tree."

Below: "Seaton Willoughby, sleuthing at Pipchippin, created a scene when he searched the pockets of all the scullery maids."

Above: "Mama opening night, in the role that made her famous."

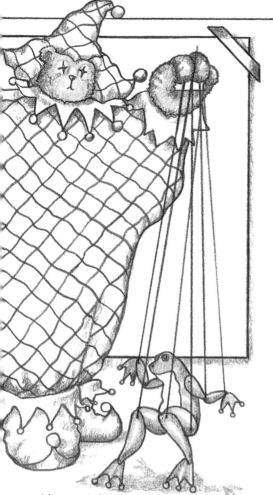

Above, right: "My Great Great Aunt and Uncle: The Countess Mirabella, inventor of the umbrella, and Baron von Burstenberg, heir to the Happy Face Balloon Fortune."

Below: "My favorite relative, 'Ducky,' Grande Duchesse of Antarctica, and the rarest of all my forebears, a polar mermaid."

Above: High-stepping at Pipchippin.

The Grande Duchesse times her journey up from the Great White South to arrive at Pipchippin on the first day of the Winter Solstice. She is the ultimate houseguest, bearing *petits cadeaux* for one and all: A little something for Mrs. Grosgrain's pouch, extravagant knickknacks for the House, a new slipcover for the Chair, ribbons and fans for the ladies in the West Wing, special spices and rare frozen blubbers for Monsieur Green-Oui to use to make succulent Antarctic specialties.

One year, she astounds everyone when she arrives with a string of musically talented penguins for her beloved little Smoothie. So the Penguin String Musicians come to Pipchippin to stay. They add a

certain something to daily life. During the day, Abiner often hears the slapping of their flippers and big feet down the endlessly long halls. When they aren't serenading Abiner, or parading through the passages, they are congregating in the Icehouse or up in the Master Bathroom, playing Slidey-Slide in the big white tub filled with cracked ice that reminds them a little bit of home.

Her Royal Duckiness is pictured here in the Spectacular underground Purple Grotto Palace she calls home, preparing to embark upon her journey northward. Seated upon her royal barge, escorted by a rare brace of star-antlered sea stags, Ducky checks her face and tells the musicians, "Snap it up, darlings. Winter's coming and my precious Abiner is expecting me."

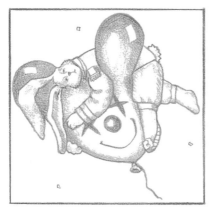

ABINER KNOWS, AS DO ALL WISE BEARS, THAT NOTHING PERKS up a long hibernation like a good party; hence, no one has ever turned down an invitation to the Annual Pipchippin Winter Ball.

On the day of the party, Abiner is relaxed. He knows that matters are well in hand. The Reynolds cubs will be trudging up faithfully from the village to help Mrs. Grosgrain handle the innumerable rafts of her special Winter Snowball Croquettes and to help Squeezy and Galeazza with the endless raven-winged tulip arrangements. The lanterns are lit, to be followed soon by the moon. Abiner sallies forth, yawning with winter wit. Wearing his best robe and slippers, he blinks at his guests as they arrive. Swell-looking in satin breeches and silk hose, Puppy is allowed to stay up late tonight. The guests troop and lumber sedately down the stairs and Abiner asks them whether they have brought gifts for Puppy. With a warm pressing of Paws, Abiner sends them into the furry glitter of Pipchippin's Great Hall on this most dazzling of all nights of the year.

Just before midnight, all eyes are drawn to the head of the enormous staircase. Trumpets blast. There is a jingling of bells and a rustle of fine furs, taffeta and trappings. Abiner knows immediately that all this excitement means the entrance of Ducky.

Finally, with everyone on their way home, Abiner lounges on the terrace and enjoys one last cookie. Pondering his good fortune—trusting friends, faithful retainers, distinctive forebears, and his loyal confidante, Puppy—Abiner asks himself, of what other comforts could this world consist? Oh, yes...cookies...in the pocket or in the paw to share with one who loves you.

"What a beautiful bear life," Abiner sighs. "This is what Grandma Bootsie would have called 'truly elegant.'"

Overleaf: A midnight cruise on Lake Pipchippin lulls Abiner and Puppy to sleep, and to dream...dreams of stars and their whispery songs...dreams of the moon and its shadowy face...dreams of you and me.

The Arms of Abiner Smoothie

The fierce polar bear twins protect the coronet of bruin aristocracy.
The salmon sailing ship signifies the earliest fishermen and seafaring explorers.

The flag on the right depicts the earliest known Smoothie in profile.

The flag on the left, the evergreen and acorn, signifies hibernation
and other autumnal pleasures. The two are bound together by the
traditional raven-winged tulip, cultivated by generations of Smoothies.

The Sea Stag is the mythological beast who travels both the underground rivers
and the heavens in search of dreams. It is the guardian of cubs.

The castle in a pastoral setting of clouds and cookies is the house of bruin domestic tranquility.

The cloven-hooved hare contemplating the heart is a sign of forest royalty,
and signifies the well known fact that bears are incurable romantics.